DISNEY·PIXAR

Cars

2

Illustrated by
Art Mawhinney and the Disney Storybook Artists

 pi kids® **publications international, ltd.**

D0471153

After another Piston Cup win, Lightning McQueen is ready for a vacation, but thanks to Mater, he'll be competing in the World Grand Prix instead! Find these things around the Wheel Well restaurant from Lightning's racing past.

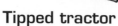

Newspaper clipping

Tipped tractor

Car boot

Picture of Doc Hudson

Can of Rust-eze

Tourists

Lightning and his crew are at Miles Axlerod's World Grand Prix party in Tokyo! Can you find these world-class cars at the party?

Finn McMissile

Fillmore

Grem

Miles Axlerod

Holley Shiftwell

Luigi

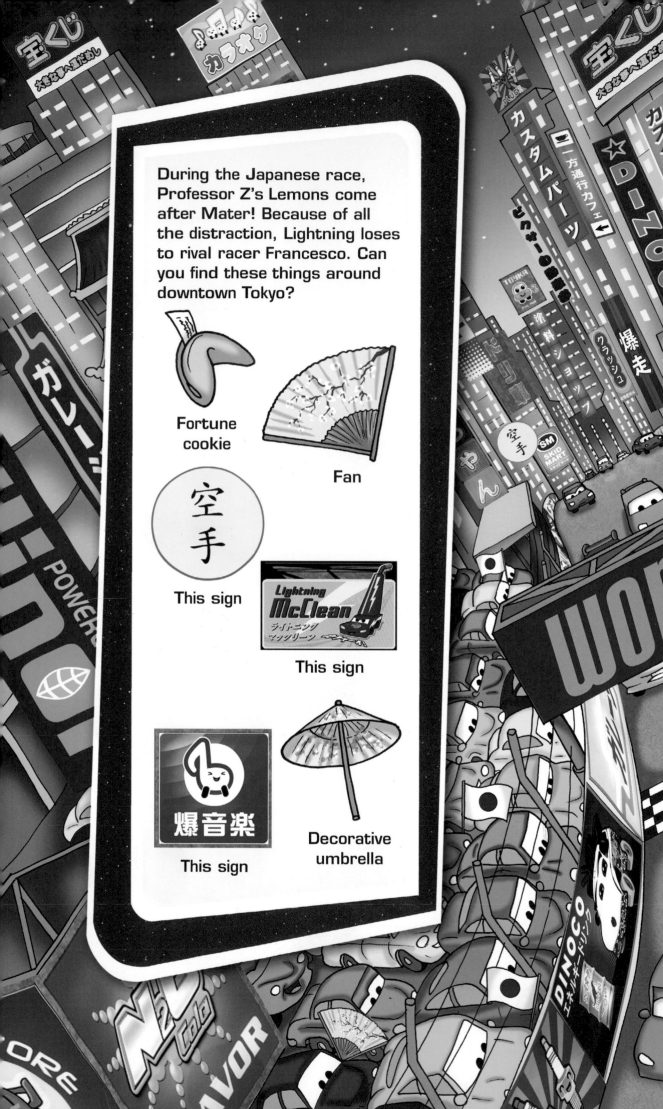

During the Japanese race, Professor Z's Lemons come after Mater! Because of all the distraction, Lightning loses to rival racer Francesco. Can you find these things around downtown Tokyo?

Fortune cookie

Fan

空手

This sign

This sign

This sign

Decorative umbrella

When Lightning says that Mater let him down, Mater decides to go home. Holley and Finn intercept him and take him to Paris. Together, the three track down an informant named Tomber. Can you find these things around Tomber's garage?

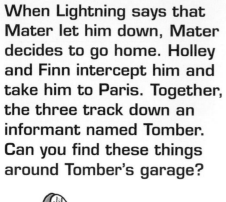

This headlight

This muffler

This hood

This windshield wiper

This tire

This bumper

It's a homecoming party for Luigi! Lightning gets advice from Luigi's Uncle Topolino. Lightning regrets that he got angry with Mater. He wants to apologize to him. Can you find these party guests?

Luigi

Guido's cousin

Aunt Topolino

Uncle Topolino

Luigi's nephew

Luigi's cousin

The Radiator Springs friends arrive in London to help Lightning and Mater! Can you find these cars fighting off Lemons?

Red

Sally

Sarge

Professor Z

Guido

Ramone

There's a bomb attached to Mater! Luckily, Mater and Lightning arrive at Buckingham Palace just in time to have Miles Axlerod disarm the device. They tell the queen that Axlerod was behind Professor Z's plan all along! Can you find these royal guards?

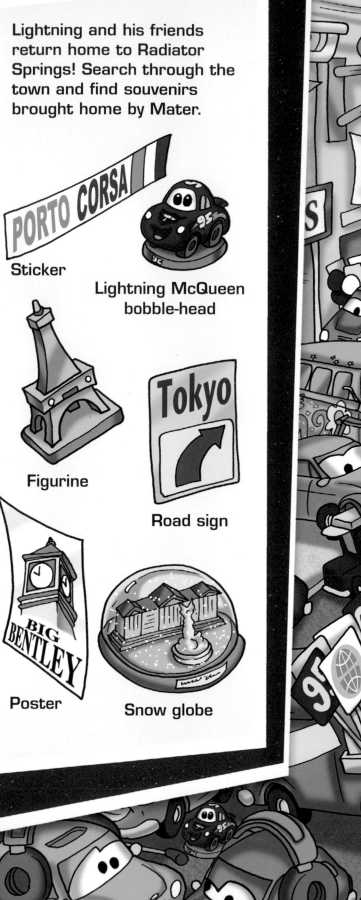

Lightning and his friends
return home to Radiator
Springs! Search through the
town and find souvenirs
brought home by Mater.

PORTO CORSA

Sticker

Lightning McQueen
bobble-head

Figurine

Tokyo

Road sign

BIG
BENTLEY

Poster

Snow globe

Lightning agrees to join the World Grand Prix! Go back to the Wheel Well restaurant and find these racing-related things.

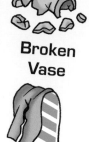

Flag

Headset

Organic fuel

Al Oft

Piston Cup

Francesco

Mater caused some destruction at Miles Axlerod's party after he gulped some wasabi! Go back and find these things that Mater ran into.

Broken Vase

Oil puddle

Crooked Mt. Fuji painting

Ripped sign

Cracked fountain

Dropped lamp

Go back to downtown Tokyo and find 10 Japanese flags.

Return to Tomber's garage and find these posters.

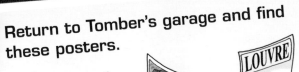

Eiffel Tower poster

Arc de Triomphe poster

Louvre poster

Notre Dame poster

Gastow's poster

The Seine River poster

Uncle Topolino tells Lightning, "Whoever finds a friend, finds a treasure." Can you find these treasures in Italy?

Gold coins

Crystal chandelier

String of pearls

Gold plaque

Bejeweled hood

Vase

Go back to the London battle and find these Lemon cars defeated by the Radiator Springs crew.

Yellow Gremlin

Orange Gremlin

Purple Hugo

Red Hugo

Rust-colored Pacer

Gray Pacer

Find these British subjects in the crowd at Buckingham Palace.

Go back to the Radiator Springs and find these tasty treats enjoyed by the crowd.

V6 smoothie

Organic fuel

Coolant

Transmission fluid

Anti-freeze

Motor oil